Fairy Sparkle's Secret Wish

Presented by Andy Pandy Playgroup

to _____ Terri _____

on

30th June 2016

igloobooks

Deep in the magical wood, the fairies were at play. All along the enchanted pathways, tiny bells **tinkled** as little fairies flew in circles...

... leaving trails of fairy dust.

Fairy Sparkle wanted to play with her friends,
but it was dusk and time for her to light the fairy lamps.

She flew between the trees, **tapping** her wand against
each lamp until they all **flickered** and **glowed** gently.

At the fairy well,
Sparkle lit the last
lamp and gave a sigh.

"I'm fed up of doing the same thing every night," she said.
"I want to do something more interesting."

Sparkle saw her friend, Twinklebell, swirling her wand around a pot of **magic!**

Twinklebell was making **fairy dust** for the other fairies.

"I **wish** I could have her job," said Sparkle, **enviously**.

Sparkle flew over to Twinklebell. **"Hello,"** said Twinklebell. **"I'm just adding a sprinkle of starlight,** then the fairy dust will be ready."

The magical mixture **whirled** around and

burst

into a cloud of fairy dust.

The two fairies darted around, catching the fairy dust.

"Thanks, Sparkle. I'll be right back. I'm just going to fetch my special bag to carry our purses," said Twinklebell, flying away.

Sparkle stared at Twinklebell's pot of magic.

"I wish I could make the fairy dust instead of Twinklebell," she sighed.

Sparkle saw something move between the trees.

"Who's there?" she gasped.

A strange woman in a dark red robe stepped forward.

"Don't be afraid, little fairy, I am your friend," said the woman, holding out her hand.

"I **heard** your magic wish,"
said the woman, with a **smile**.
"**YOU** can be the maker of the
fairy dust if you want to be."

Sparkle **flapped** her wings, excitedly. "**How?**" she asked.

"Tell your friend that
the fairy queen has
a **special** job for
her to do," said
the woman.

"You want me to lie?" asked Sparkle.

"Oh, no," said the woman. "It's just a little fib. That doesn't count as a lie."

Sparkle **really** wanted to make the fairy dust, so she decided to tell the fib. She flew away from the **strange** woman.

"I **must** go and find Twinklebell," she said,

searching for her friend in the forest.

Sparkle found Twinklebell by a stream. "The fairy queen has a special job for you to do," lied Sparkle. Twinklebell was curious. "I had better go straight away," she said, fluttering off.

Sparkle **whizzed** to the magic pot and **sprinkled** glittery magic inside. Nothing seemed to work.

"**Why can't I make the fairy dust?**" she asked.

"**Don't worry,**" said the woman in the red cloak. "**Let ME help you.**"

The woman took out her wand and muttered something under her breath. Sparkle watched as the woman tipped a bottle of green liquid into the pot.

The magic mixture **boiled** and **hissed**, forming a **glittering**, green cloud.

"What are you doing?" asked Sparkle. "That doesn't look like fairy dust."

"It isn't," said the woman, removing her cloak and revealing her black dress and purple wings.

"Your wish to betray your friend brought me here. Then, you broke the fairy law by telling a lie. I am the dark witch and because of you, all of Fairyland is now under MY control."

Sparkle was frightened.

She was about to dart off when the witch cast a **wicked** spell and caught her.

"STOP!" cried a voice.

Sparkle looked up to see the fairy queen flying towards them.

"YOU don't belong in Fairyland, witch. Leave Sparkle alone, or I will use MY fairy magic against you."

The dark witch **cackled**. She stepped forward, raising her arm. **"Draw your wand,** queen of the fairies," said the dark witch. **"We will see whose magic is the strongest."**

"**Fairyland is mine!**" cried the dark witch and a **blast** of lightning shot out of her wand.

The fairy queen raised her wand and a bright **flash** of light surrounded the witch.

"**NOOOO!**" screamed the witch, as she **burst** into a thousand sparkles of light and disappeared forever.

Fairyland was saved!

All the fairies **fluttered** around in excitement, **clapping** and **cheering**. "Thank you, Fairy Queen," they said. "We'll never have to worry about the witch, ever again."

Sparkle hugged Twinklebell.

"I'm so sorry I told a lie," said Sparkle.

"I promise I won't betray you again."

Twinklebell smiled at her. "You've learned your lesson, Sparkle," she said. "I forgive you."

All was **just** as it should be in Fairyland.